# SUN AND STC

CW00429012

SPONSORED BY HSBC BANK PLC

# SUN AND STORM

## AND OTHER STORIES

Carolyn Watcyn

I    Jenny

Gyda'm dymuniadau gorau
a chofion annwyl,

Carolyn

GEE & SON (Denbigh) Ltd.

Translated from the original *Haul a Drycin*
by Kate Roberts,
first published December 1981

ISBN 0 7074 0347 2

*Introduction by Professor Gwyn Thomas*
*Art work by Sir Kyffin Williams, OBE, RA*

*Printed and Published by*
**GEE AND SON (DENBIGH) LTD.**
**Chapel Street, Denbigh LL16 3SW**

For

CATHERINE AND SARAH

With Love

# Contents

# Acknowledgements

I am grateful to Dr. Kate Roberts for allowing me to make this translation. When I asked her permission to translate her book, she told me I was being a bit of a nuisance expecting her to write letters at her age, but to go ahead provided Professor Gwyn Thomas approved!

I am therefore especially grateful to him for his support and for all the time and care he has given to this project.

I would also like to thank most warmly Sir Kyffin Williams O.B.E., R.A., for so kindly allowing me to use his work to make the book beautiful; and my daughter Catherine for all her patience and skill in making the text presentable.

My thanks and love to my mother Joan and my late father John Watkin-Jones, and my grandparents Catherine and Edward Richardes, my daughters Catherine and Sarah and all my family for their love and support always; also to Dr Peter Griffiths, Ann Roberts, Judith and Malcolm Stammers, Nan Hughes, Denise Morris; and to all my wonderful friends.

I am grateful also to the late Professor Bedwyr Lewis Jones and the staff of the Department of Welsh, and to Mr Alwyn Roberts, LL.B., M.A., and the staff of the Centre for Continuing Education at the University of Wales, Bangor, who have been so kind and helpful always.

I very much appreciate the assistance of Mr T. Alun Williams of Gwasg Gee, and of Mr Adrian Jones and Mr Walter Roberts of HSBC who have made this publication possible. Many thanks to them too.

CAROLYN

# Introduction

Kate Roberts is, justifiably, regarded as one of the most accomplished writers of Welsh prose of the twentieth century. She was born in 1891 and was brought up in Rhosgadfan, a village in the quarrying and small farming uplands that rise from the bay of Caernarfon. At the end of the nineteenth century and for the greater part of the first half of the twentieth century this part of Wales was entirely Welsh-speaking. Kate Roberts' writing shows a very sensitive person's unerring feeling for words used by a society whose monolinguism provided them with a copiousness of Welsh that is difficult to find its equal today. This inherited wealth of language was reinforced in her case by the disciplined thoroughness of her Welsh course at the University of North Wales, Bangor. Like many Welsh graduates of her generation she became a school teacher and taught mainly in schools in South Wales. After she had married Morris T. Williams in 1928 they bought the Gee Press in Denbigh. After his death in 1946 she heroically kept that business going for ten years, when it was sold. During that time she was a mainstay of the press's weekly newspaper, *Y Faner ac Amserau Cymru*. She died, honoured and old, in 1985.

A substantial part of Kate Roberts' work - short stories and novels - deals with the society of her upbringing in north Wales. Another part of it deals with the period of the Depression in south Wales, and yet another part deals with the lives of people in a mid- to late-twentieth century suburbia. The parts referred to in this rough division of her

11

work do not represent an ordered chronology of their composition - she reverted to her early society in some of her later work. The society in the first two parts (which do not represent the actual chronology of their composition) has, on the whole, a certain kind of heroism; for the most part, individuals face up to the harshness of their everyday lives with a strong sense of moral values provided by their Nonconformist religion. And they manage to fashion a kind of happiness out of circumstances that seem unpropitious. Suburbia, later on, has largely lost any feeling for the old Nonconformist values, and the lives of individuals have less direction, and they are more neurotic.

The short stories translated here were first published as a volume in Welsh in 1981. The translator's Notes make it clear that the stories in which Winni appear deal with the development of a character already familiar to Welsh readers from other books by Kate Roberts. Although such stories are among the latest that Kate Roberts published, the period is that of the author's early childhood. So it is in the story entitled "Starting to Live". "Emptiness" is almost biographical and provides a diary of an old woman's feelings in the late twentieth century. "Maggie" is also a story set in the latter half of the twentieth-century, in some suburbia.

The writing in these stories is one of an almost elemental simplicity, which is skilfully conveyed in this translation. The stories themselves present girls or women at different stages in their lives. They present various aspects of femininity at various times. The ingrained attitudes and values of Kate Roberts' upbringing and of her own personality are presented in these stories and may seem old-fashioned to many modern readers, but the portrayals of women are, in some ways, features of a modern, self-assertive feminism. Which, in a writer of almost ninety years of age, brought up in a male-dominated society (though not a male-dominated home), is remarkable.

All Nonconformist Welsh readers of a certain age will recognize aspects of behaviour that Kate Roberts applauds as virtues. Good women, especially, are honest; clean, in house and person; industrious; providers of nourishing if simple food, expertly prepared - and they appreciate the occasional scram; they can adapt and, if need be, patch old clothes for new purposes; they are also often strong women - Begw's mother is such a woman. The bad women are the opposite: they are slobs, and are dirty, lazy and wasteful - though even the worst may have some hidden virtue: Lisi Jên, Winni's stepmother, an archetypal slut, can make excellent pastry. The bad men are poor workers, unmindful of their children, and drunkards. These days, these lists of virtues and vices seem almost parodic. At one time, and that a hard time, the virtues listed were necessary to make life possible. They were, for Kate Roberts, values that made for an unexpected heroism. The fact that so many of her virtues and the virtues of the society in which she was brought up have been cast aside is a reflection of the great social changes that occurred during her lifetime.

GWYN THOMAS

*Chapter 1*

# A Maid's Anxiety

The waves lapped quietly against the edge of the quay wall. The gulls flew about crying harshly and then strutted pompously on the quay itself. Winni sat daydreaming on the wall, holding tightly the handle of the push-chair, in which sat Robert, the son of her master and mistress. He was playing with his rag dog, shouting occasionally and throwing the dog out. Whenever he did so, Winni picked up the dog and gave it back to him. Everywhere was quiet, the quay was deserted during this hour between lunch and tea.

Then a boy appeared, about eighteen or twenty years old, and sat cheekily on the wall beside Winni. She got up immediately and started to move away with the push-chair.

'No', he said, 'you're not going off like that.'

'Yes I am', she said, 'my mistress is expecting me.'

The boy wore a starched double collar and shoes, things which Winni, in her country way, despised. The country boys wore boots and soft single collars.

'I want to talk to you', he said, 'I want you to come for a walk with me.'

'Go home to your mother for a dummy, you wet calf.'

'What's a calf? Baby cow is it?'

'I'm telling you again, go home to your mother and learn to speak properly.'

Just then, who should come past but her master, and the baby started to shout joyfully, 'Dad, Dad.'

'You'd better go home Winni,' he said.

And that was that. Winni blushed and a pain came to her breast. She thought how awkward it was, her master coming past just at the moment when she was resisting the boy's advances with her strongest language – well, almost her strongest language. It was likely that she would have sworn at him, had they continued to talk. She knew that her mistress would hold her responsible. And that was how it was.

'Winni, Mr. Hughes saw you talking to some boy on the quay just now.'

'Yes Ma'm, but I couldn't help it.'

'You're too young to be talking to boys.'

'I was sitting on the quay wall holding tightly onto the handle of the push-chair when this boy came along and sat down by me.'

Just then the master came in.

'Yes, Winni', he said, 'what did he want?'

'He wanted me to go for a walk with him.'

'And what did you say?'

'I gave him a proper telling off and told him to go home to his mother. I did everything except swear at him.'

The master smiled. Mrs. Hughes went on.

'Had you seen him before? It seems strange to me that he should ask that if it was the first time you'd seen him.'

'Yes, indeed Mrs. Hughes.'

The master broke in.

'I can easily believe that, I know his family. Real scum'

The mistress went on.

'You see Winni. I could easily send you home from here.'

At this Winni burst into tears.

'But honestly, Mrs. Hughes, I couldn't help it. And please don't send me home. My father would give me a hiding and perhaps throw me out. I'm so happy here with little Robert.'

The master said.

'Don't be too cross with her Mary. You know Winni's a good maid, a lot better than the others who've been here. It would be a great pity to lose her.'

'Yes, I know that. We'll see. Go and start getting tea Winni.'

Winni did not sleep much that night. She saw herself thrown out of her work, and because of that, failing to find another place. She saw her father giving her a beating and throwing her out, and her without anywhere to go. She went through things over and over again as she lay in bed, and came to a dead end with ever increasing worry.

On the following day, Saturday, she had the afternoon off, and she would go home, but only because of little Sionyn. She would not dare tell her father and Lisi-Jên about her trouble. She would have to pretend to be cheerful, something she was used to doing since her father brought a second wife home.

She decided to get up early and wash Robert's clothes before washing up the breakfast dishes. As usual her master gave her a shilling to pay for the brake.

Lisi-Jên had given the place a lick and a promise, and her father had changed and was on the point of leaving for the town. Sionyn gave her a great welcome and insisted on sitting on her knee to have tea. The tea was good, her step-mother had made a blackberry tart.

But Winni sensed an atmosphere in the house. Her father and his wife were not speaking to each other.

They had obviously been quarrelling. He had been giving her the sharp edge of his tongue as he used to do to Winni's mother. When Winni started to leave, Sionyn sobbed and cried, and she began to cry too. The child did not have much to make him happy. His clothes were shabby and he had few toys. She felt sorry for him. When she came to earn a bit more money she would buy him toys and new clothes. At the moment she needed new clothes badly enough herself. Her master had said that her father would not get hold of her wages. He would give her wages to her mistress and ask her to spend them on clothes for Winni.

Winni decided to go for a walk to the mountain. She felt a kind of nostalgia for the time when she and Begw had crossed it, although that had not really been a good time. But she did not have this worry on her mind then.

The mountain was russet with the colours of autumn, the stream was flowing quietly, monotonously, the water clear. The sun was on the point of setting, like a red ball, and was throwing a flush of colour onto the sea. How much she would have enjoyed all this if she were without this weight on her mind. She sat beside the small stream and began to cry again. She longed for her mother. If she were alive she could have told her all her trouble, and her mother would have said, 'Never mind, I'll keep you at home. There's plenty of work for you, and you can go to night school and chapel meetings.'

A man came down the mountain, an old neighbour, a sack of kindling on his back and a sheepdog at his side. He sat on the bank of the stream, and the dog too.

'Hello, Winni, how are you after all this while?'

'Very well thank you, Huw Tomos, and you?'

'Fine thanks. How's it going in the town there?'

'Alright, I'm very happy, I've got a very good place. There's a lovely little boy there, about two years old.'

The dog listened as if he understood everything, and Winni noticed his kindly eyes, so different from her father's and step-mother's eyes this afternoon, and so like Sionyn's eyes.

She decided to go and see Elin Gruffydd, Begw's mother, and tell her everything. Immediately her worry vanished and she felt peace of mind.

The mist started to creep over the mountain and reached her. It formed drops like dew on her hair. She got up and said goodbye to the man and the dog.

'Come in Winni. What's the matter? You've been crying.'

'Yes, I'm in trouble, and I went to the mountain. I was longing for my mother, because of this trouble I'm in.'

'What's the matter? You surely haven't disobeyed your mistress?'

'No, not at all.'

'I'm glad to hear that.'

Winni told her story, and Begw listened, her mouth open and her eyes wide. When Winni came to her exchange with the boy, the 'wet calf' and so on, the two others laughed.

'It may sound funny now, but it wasn't funny at the time. I managed to stop myself swearing at him, and a good thing I did, because who came past but the master.'

'He would have to come past just then', said Elin Gruffydd.

'But I couldn't help it. There I was, trying to explain to them in the house afterwards.'

'Were they cross?'

'Oh no, but my mistress sort of hinted that she might give me the sack.'

'For a little thing like that?'

'That's what I thought, and that's what's been worrying me since yesterday.'

'Did you tell your father?'

'Oh heavens no. He'd have given me a hiding and thrown me out, and where would I go then?'

'Here,' said Elin Gruffydd and Begw together.

'Oh thank you, that's a relief.'

'I don't think your mistress will send you away if you please her Winni.'

'Well, the master said that I'm a better maid than the others they've had before, and he gave me a shilling to pay for the brake.'

'There you are. That's good. You'll see, everything will be alright. It's very hard to get a good young girl for low wages these days, especially where there's a child or children. Cheer up Winni. Let's have a bite to eat.'

And the three of them had tea, with a boiled egg each.

Winni was much happier in the brake, going back to town. She would not be left with no-where to go. Elin Gruffydd would be sure to find her another place.

When she arrived back she was surprised to see bright lights everywhere. Her mistress came to meet her in the hall, holding Robert by the hand. The boy should have been in bed.

'Robert has refused to go to bed until you got back Winni. And thank you for washing his clothes. I ironed them this afternoon.'

'We'll have supper in the basement tonight so as to keep upstairs clean for tomorrow. We'll all go to chapel tomorrow morning, and Robert can come with us.'

She smiled welcomingly.

'And from now on we'll all go like that to chapel every Sunday morning.'

*Chapter 2*

# Sun and Storm

The whole family went to chapel on Sunday morning, Mr. and Mrs. Hughes, Robert, the little boy and Winni the maid. After a day of anxiety for Winni, thinking that she would lose her place after being caught speaking to one of the town boys, it was evident that it was not her mistress's intention to turn her away.

The day before when the maid was visiting her home in the country Mrs. Hughes had been thinking about Winni's clothes. They were very few. She had the same coat and the same frock to go out with Robert in the afternoon that she had to go to chapel, clothes that some woman in the country had altered to fit Winni, and they were old things anyway.

So her mistress had set about looking through her own wardrobe the night before, and had found an old coat and old frock. They were not so very old fashioned although they were over six years old. She tried them on Winni on Sunday morning and they fitted exactly. The frock was of one colour - dark red - and the coat the colours of autumn. Winni looked very pretty in them; she was very tall for her age. She had a cap that would go with the clothes. Then Mrs. Hughes wondered whether it would be better for Winni to put up her hair, although she was rather young for that. She plaited it for her and tied it with a dark red ribbon.

Winni was very happy going to chapel. She knew by now that she would not have to leave her place. Although she did not usually go to chapel when she was at home, because she had no suitable clothes, she was looking forward to the service, and her mistress's clothes gave her a good feeling, the feeling of warmth (the weather had turned cold) and the feeling of having something new to wear.

She was not able to sing in the chapel because she did not know the tunes, and the sermon was something strange to her. She could not understand it very well because she had been brought up like a heathen after her mother died. This life was so strange to her! It was more than moving from the country to the town; it was moving from one way of life to another, from an uncivilised life to a civilised one. She tended to look about her and see the people, so different from her in their smart clothes. She concentrated on the preacher for a while, admiring his good looks.

Then she noticed a young girl sitting in front of her, a girl about eighteen years old she thought. She was dressed prettily in a blue coat and grey hat. She had wavy, honey coloured hair, which fell in curls on her neck. She could not take her eyes off her. On the way out, this girl turned to Winni and asked,

'How are you? You're the one who has come to Mr. and Mrs. Hughes the Corner Shop aren't you?'

'Yes.'

'My name is Gwen Edwards. I've been with Mr. and Mrs. Rogers at Oaklands for three years. I believe your name is Winni.'

'Yes, Winni Ifans.'

'I've heard about you. Have you got friends here in the town?'

'No.'

'Would you like to come for a walk with me one evening or Saturday afternoon?'

'Thanks very much. But I'm not allowed out at night, and I go home every Saturday afternoon.'

'We'll have to try and arrange something.'

Winni admired this girl with her warm brown eyes and her friendly face. On her way back to the house she felt like a different girl, not just because of her clothes. She was, it seemed likely, on her way to making a friend. Circumstances had never before allowed her to make one. It was true that Begw was very faithful to her, but Begw was a child compared with her. She felt that she was on the point of a great change. She was no longer the daughter of Twm Ffinni Hadog, but a girl living in a comfortable home and on the point of making friends with someone a bit older than herself, and someone likeable too. At that moment she did not care about her father or Lisi-Jên. She could snap her fingers at them. It was true that Sionyn had a special place in her heart, but she would have to break away from him sometime, if she could. That was the big question. She had given him all her affection. He would grow up and she would become a woman. Woman! She could not imagine herself a woman, and yet, leaving chapel this morning, she felt that she was no longer a child.

Two Saturdays later Gwen and Winni went together for a walk into the country. Neither of them had any money to finish their journey with a cup of tea in a cafe, but the two of them had enough imagination to enjoy the colours and scents of nature on the footpaths. They both told each other their life history.

Gwen had already heard a little of Winni's background before this encounter. She knew that she had lost her mother and that she had a useless lazy step-mother, and that her father got drunk on Saturday nights, but she did not know

23

that Winni was forced to rely on other people for her clothing, yes, even for a bit of kindness.

'I've lost my father too', said Gwen, 'and I have two brothers who haven't started work yet, so I had to go into service. I've been with Mrs. Rogers since I was fourteen. I'm eighteen now.'

'I'm nearly fourteen', said Winni.

'Do you like your place?'

'Yes, there's plenty of work there, but I get good food.'

'And me.'

Now, there was one thing which had been on Gwen's mind since she met Winni that Sunday morning - and since she had heard a little of her history. She wondered whether her step-mother had taught her some of the facts of life, about the thing which would happen to her soon if it had not already happened. She struggled with herself, wondering whether she should tell her now before it was too late.

'Winni, forgive me for asking you something very private. Has your step-mother taught you anything about — ? Well, it was her duty to tell you one thing at the age you are now.'

'Lisi Jên doesn't know what duty is. What is this thing?'

'It's like this Winni, there'll soon be a big change your body.'

Then Gwen went on to explain to Winni about this change in her life in detail, without hiding anything, and indicated to her what she would have to have to make herself comfortable. She promised to give her some of the necessary things as she knew that Winni had no money with which to buy them.

Winni was frightened and began to cry.

'Don't cry Winni, it happens to every girl. It has to happen or there would be something wrong with you. You'll be ill if it doesn't happen.'

Winni's feelings were very mixed as she walked back to the house that evening. She had enjoyed her walk with Gwen, but had been shaken by the new knowledge. She had a sharp bout of longing for Sionyn too.

She mentioned Gwen's talk to her mistress. It was a relief to tell someone, and Mrs. Hughes, said,

'I was on the point of telling you about it. Don't worry, I'll look after everything for you when the time comes.'

'If my mother were alive she would have taught me.'

Winni was worried about the whole business as she put Robert to bed. Yes, life was broadening for her. She was a different girl tonight from the one she had been last night. One thing which surprised her was that Begw's mother had not mentioned these things to her, but then Begw had been in every time she called, and her mother would not have ventured to speak of things like this in front of a child.

She spent the evening reading that night, since she was home early, but she could not concentrate. The events of the afternoon went through her head like a tune repeating itself. Yet, an occasional feeling of happiness came to her when she remembered Gwen.

Then, in the middle of the quietness there was the sound of loud banging on the front door. She went nervously to open it. She nearly had a fit when she saw her father there, reeling drunk. He could hardly stand on his feet. He shouted.

'You've got to come home, this is no place for you, you should be at home with Lisi-Jên.'

At this Mr. Hughes came along the hall.

'Get out, Twm Ifan this is no place for you either.'

'Yes. I want this girl to come home now. The wife is expecting again, there'll be more work there, and she'll have to have help in the house. And I want her money now.'

'Look here. Twm Ifan, it's up to Winni to say if she wants

25

to come home or not. As for her money, you'll not see a penny of that. She's got to have clothes.'

'No, I'm not coming home', said Winni with a sob, 'I'd rather go to jail.'

'I'm taking you with me now, you bloody bitch, I've got the right, you're under age.'

'None of that language,' broke in Mr. Hughes.

Winni ran to the stairs and up to the bedroom. Her father started after her but he fell with a crash over the mat. Mr. Hughes helped him up and pushed him unceremoniously into the street. Mrs. Hughes arrived there, having heard the commotion, and asked where was Winni. She went up to the bedroom and found her there lying on her bed sobbing bitterly.

'Don't cry Winni, Mr. Hughes will deal with your father.'

Winni stopped crying and came down to supper, shyly, because her master and mistress had seen her father as he was, worse than one of the scum of the town. Mr. Hughes was quiet and thoughtful, his hand under his chin. Presently he said.

'I'll go to the solicitor on Monday, and I'll find out whether your father has a right to take you from here.'

'Thank you very much Mr. Hughes.'

Winni was able to sleep all night. She believed that things would come right in the end. For a while she wanted to go far enough away so that her father could not come near her. But she did not have enough money to be able to pay for her train fare and other things. She had no choice. She had mentioned going to jail. In one sense she was in prison already. But she had made a good friend. She could tell her worries to Gwen now, and her master and mistress were kind enough. And there was her master, going to see the solicitor. She hoped that he would be able to do something to stop her father from forcing her to go home.

On Monday evening Mr. Hughes explained to his wife the result of his visit to the solicitor.

'I saw Mr. Rogers himself – I told him Winni's history, how she had lost her mother, how her father had remarried to a lazy slut. How they have one child, and Winni was forced to do a great deal of work instead of her step-mother. The father drinking. Winni neglected, never getting new clothes, and suffering from the cold. Other people providing her with clothes. Her father taking her wages to spend on drink. Mr. Rogers listened keenly, without his face showing anything, but I knew that his brain was working. He asked me why I was so concerned about the girl. I said it was because she is such a good maid, better than others we've had before, and also because I feel sorry for her.'

Mrs. Hughes listened attentively.

'Then he said that her father has a right to take her home, but he does not have a right to neglect her. So, if he were to take her home a case of cruelty could be brought against him. Then he seemed to reconsider. Another case could be brought against him too. He has been in our house drunk and disorderly, causing a disturbance and using indecent language. Mr. Rogers is going to write a strong letter to him, charging him with the two things and saying that if he comes near our house again, or thinks of taking the girl home, a case will be brought against him in the court.'

When she had heard these things, the sun came again into Winni's life.

## Chapter 3

# Oh! Winni! Winni!

A December morning in a basement in the town; the gas light hissing like a snake all the time; the sound of people walking on the pavement outside and banging the grating like a child striking one note on the piano all day, and Winni trying to please her mistress by cleaning the flues of the big old double-ovened stove. It would be easier to do this if Robert, the four year old child were to stay with his mother on the floor above. But he would insist on being with Winni, and by now there was the same amount of soot on both their faces. Her mistress wanted the stove to work perfectly for the great Christmas baking. When asked to do it by her mistress Winni had half refused.

'Why don't you ask that Mrs. Jones who comes here to clean on Friday morning to do it?'

'Now, Winni, that's no way to talk. Say - 'Mrs. Jones' not 'that Mrs. Jones who comes here to clean.' You know her well enough by now.'

'There are hundreds of Mrs. Joneses living in this town.'

'Yes, but there's only one who comes here to clean.'

'Who's going to show me how to do it?'

'Like this, look.'

And her mistress took hold of one of the flues with the tips of her fingers and pulled it out.

'You have to put the brush up that hole there, as far as you can, and the soot will come down that way.'

She did not do anything, except point to 'that way' as she had dirtied her fingers.

'And then take the soot outside and put it in the dustbin.'

So the morning had come, and Winni, not much the wiser for the pointing directions of her mistress, had followed her instinct with the brush, and frequently her arm had followed the brush further than necessary, and had come out the same colour as the brush. But the soot had come down smoothly like black flour, plenty of it, and having come from there, had descended low enough for Robert to get his hands into it. Having taken the soot outside she was now blackleading the stove; her face pouring with sweat, and from pushing away the lock of hair which kept falling over her eyes, her face was like the face of a black man.

That was how her mistress saw her when she came down to see if she had finished. When she saw Winni and the boy she stood in the doorway and exclaimed: 'W-ell,' under her breath. She seized the boy and took him, screaming, to the bedroom leaving Winni to shift for herself as best she could. Winni wanted to escape to somewhere, even to Lisi Jên. But she carried on, she boiled water on the gas stove; she washed herself and used the water to wash the hearthstone, hoping that it would take more time to wash Robert upstairs than she had taken to wash. She boiled more water while she was lighting the fire, and washed the floor of the kitchen; she cleaned away the kitchen dust and put back the mats. She put on a clean apron and sat in the chair to think.

Which was better, collecting soot from the big old stove, or living with Lisi Jên in a mess of a kitchen? A year ago she was shivering in school in a cold classroom with a smoky stove in it which would not draw properly. At least this stove was drawing well; the wood crackling in its heart and the flames blazing up the chimney. She had one other choice, to walk about on the mountain; but she could not do that now when the mist would be shrouding its peak, and would drip dew onto the locks of her hair, and the marshy places suck down her clogs. There was no cotton grass waving, no flowering heather, or stagshorn moss to be plucked now. London would be no better; there were dark basements and gas and stoves there too.

The trials of life were closing in on her. But she remembered one spot of light, Elin Gruffydd's kitchen; and Sionyn too, with his dirty overall, throwing things into the fire and running out to the rubbish pit with a crust in his hand. There was no-one to run and wash him when he fell into the rubbish pit. In the middle of her day-dreaming her mistress came down. She looked around the kitchen, but said nothing about the brightness of the stove nor about the tidiness.

'Better start getting dinner now Winni.'

'The stove hasn't heated up yet.'

'It will have by the time you peel the potatoes and wash the cabbage, and you can start the meat off on the other stove. We'll have fruit instead of a pudding today.'

There was no peace to think about mist, or rain, or blue sky, or sunshine, or flowers, or moss. She got going once again, and her spirits rose as she looked at the clean kitchen and knew that it was she who was to thank for that. She would have liked to sit in the kitchen all afternoon, with her hands clasped; doing nothing but looking at it and thinking of this Christmas at home. Begw would enjoy doing that; she had a home in which she could look forward to spending the day. But Twm, Winni's father, would stay in bed to recover from his drinking of the previous night. Lisi Jên would be scraping a dinner together, her husband's cap on her head, and wearing a dirty old apron. But there would be no need for Winni to work if she herself did not feel like it. That was one advantage of having a lazy slut for a step-mother.

She had no more day-dreaming in her clean kitchen in the afternoon; she had to take Robert for a walk, run some errands, come back to make tea and supper, and then do the ironing until bed time. Her master brought the supper dishes on a tray from the bedroom, and unlike his wife, showed his appreciation at seeing the kitchen so clean. That was enough for Winni to live on until Christmas; an encouragement to her to chop the suet, clean the fruit, wash the furniture and wax it.

On Christmas Eve when Winni stepped out of the door all these things had been done, and she had half a crown in her hand, her master's Christmas present, the only half crown that she had ever held in her hand, knowing that it was her own. Her father had insisted on having all her Michaelmas wages without giving her so much as a pocket handkerchief. She was happily tired; she could have slept on Lisi Jên's hard straw mattress. Before finally closing the door she looked cautiously to the left and right in case her father was hanging about. She knew he and his friends would come down to town to go drinking. She walked proudly and confidently into a toy shop to buy a present for Sionyn, and she found in the midst of the dolls and little horses a little donkey who nodded his head just as in the rhyme which she would recite to her half-brother so often to keep him happy, and he would shout 'again' all the time.

> 'The donkey lifted his head
> High up towards the sky,
> All the people gave a great cry
> Halleluiah. for ever and aye.'

As she came out she put the change into her handkerchief, her only purse; but she did not know that a pair of eyes were watching her keenly from the other side of the street. The next minute there was a hand grabbing the handkerchief from her, it was her father's hand: she could do nothing but open her mouth in surprise. When she realised what had happened she started to run after him, intending to hit him, but she heard the voice of Elin Gruffydd telling her to try and please her mistress, and if she came to know that she had been fighting in the street with her father, she would never be able to go back, nor to another place either. When she realised the depth of her disappointment she began to sob bitterly. When she saw people beginning to gather round her she ran down the street and dried her tears on the sleeve of her coat. She walked without stopping, and with every step on the pavement she called down vengeance on her father. With the one and sixpence change she had intended to buy a handkerchief for Begw and a purse for herself in which to keep the few pennies which she hoped someday to have. A man came up to her who came from the same district as herself, whom she knew by sight, but whose name she did not know.

'What's the matter Winni'

She told him her troubles.

'Here you are,' he said, and put a shilling in her hand, you can buy something with that; run before the shops close.'

She went, and she bought a handkerchief for Begw for three pence, a little purse for herself for sixpence, and put the three pence change into the purse, and the purse safely in the pocket of her frock. The man was waiting for her when she came out of the shop.

'I'll take you to the brake,' he said, 'it's not right for a girl your age to go home in the brake with those drunks. I've come to town to see my sister who's ill and I see a chance of a lift home.'

'Thank you so much, and don't tell my father you've given me anything.'

'No fear of that.'

Her disappointment was eased. Her heart warmed to people like this man, her master, and Begw's family.

The brake and its horses stood like some dark whale in a lonely corner of the square, and only the driver's hat was to be seen, his head having sunk into his collar.

'Cold night', he said through the collar of his overcoat.

The men came ambling in no great haste from the pubs; some of them swaying about like ships sailing on a turbulent sea. One tried to get into the driver's seat and fell as he tried. Someone picked him up and set him there. One tried to come and sit by Winni's side and put his hand round her waist. She gave him a shove so that he fell neatly into the opposite seat, and the friend who had helped came and sat by her side. It was enough that their knees were bumping into each other, without having to endure stinking breath by her face. Her father was among the most drunken of them, and he went to sleep with his chin on his breast.

As they left the town and its lights depression came over Winni again. The lights of the town were sad things; they were there to light the way for the feet of the people who were hurrying home from meetings; they made people's faces look grey, as if they had just been weeping, or as if they were yearning for something which they could not have, as she was herself. It is true that some people would be laughing and playing about under the lights, lovers, but she would have to pass them, to go into the house and make supper, not stay with them. The lights were sadder now, seen from the brake at the top of the hill, as if they burned for no-one but themselves in their loneliness. The distinction between the land and the Menai Straits had disappeared, and made the countryside one dark blue patch. Looking at the hills where her home was the lights seemed sadder than ever, like corpse candles, or 'glow worms' as the children of the area called them, and there was a veil of mist over them.

Some of the men gave a burst of song occasionally, 'My Grandma's Old Stick', 'The Little Thatched Cottage', and 'I Remember Now So Clearly.' Then they became quiet, closing their eyes: some were vomiting on the floor. And the horses were continuing to walk and trot, and the back of the driver's neck was moving from side to side like the fast moving pendulum of a clock measuring the rhythm of their travelling. That was all on the occasional quiet parts of the journey, then a burst of song came again, and Winni was watching the whole thing as if she were sitting on a seat in a strange land.

Having thanked the man who had helped her once again, Winni left the brake quickly and went to Elin Gruffydd's house, her father being too unsteady to take any notice of her. She went into the welcoming light, and 'How are you Winni?'. The first thing she did was to drop into a chair and cry. Begw was the first to run to her. When Winni raised her head she saw a clean table and supper on it; Robin and John Gruffydd were sitting by the table, and Elin Gruffydd by the baby's cradle rocking it. She told them again what had happened; the listeners here understood, and showed it by shaking their heads and making comments.

'Come to the table Winni, and have a bit of food', said Elin Gruffydd, and John can take you home.'

'I don't want to go home.'

'You'd better go, that's the best way,' said the father, 'or your father will come here and cause trouble, and it will be easier for you to go home tonight than tomorrow. Remember that Sionyn will be expecting you.'

Winni cheered up a bit at that.

'And you're coming here for tea tomorrow,' said Elin Gruffydd, 'and bring Sionyn with you.'

She thanked them and brought out the handkerchief and gave it to Begw.

'Oh, thank you very much,' and Begw ran to the drawer to fetch some treacle toffee for Winni.

Winni gave the handkerchief to Begw as a lady gives a gift to a child, and Begw gave the toffee to her as a mortal to a god.

'You shouldn't spend your money on Begw,' said the mother.

'You've all been so kind, I don't know how to thank you for the toffee Begw. I can eat it in bed tonight.'

When John Gruffydd and Winni arrived at Twm's house, he and Lisi Jên were eating their supper of sausages, and the frying pan had not been put away, but was still on the hob. Twm began indignantly.

'Oh, that's where she's been is it. Why the hell don't you mind your own business?'

'That's what I am doing Twm, it's my business and everyone else's if I see someone mistreated. This child isn't getting fair play. You didn't give her a penny of her own wages, and here you are stealing her bit of a 'Christmas box'.

'I had a perfect right to both, she's my child.'

'Nobody would think that from the way you treat her.'

'You and your wife are interfering too much for anyone else to have a chance to do anything for her.'

'You're putting the cart before the horse Twm. I don't know how she would have looked going into service if Elin hadn't tidied her up a bit.'

Through all this Lisi Jên was enjoying her supper, without taking her eyes off it, like someone sleeping through thunder and lighting. After John Gruffydd had

35

gone, Winni went to bed, without anyone having offered her supper. She found a piece of ribbon in a drawer in the bedroom: she threaded her purse on it and tied it round her neck. What a surprise, Lisi Jên had put clean clothes on the bed. She curled up beside Sionyn and put a piece of Begw's toffee in her mouth. She went to sleep with a sigh, but she was able to sleep without being troubled by fleas.

Sometime during the night Sionyn woke up.

'Hey, Winni, I want a present.'

He nudged her in case she had not heard him.

'Who told you you're going to get a present?'

'Mam.'

'Where did she think I'd get money from to buy a present for anyone?'

No answer.

'Nobody can buy anything with nothing. Go to sleep.'

He began to cry.

'Go to sleep. Perhaps a fairy will have brought you something by morning. I know that it's come.'

Winni woke before daybreak. She thought that the only thing she could do to kill the time before she could go to Elin Gruffydd's house would be to work. She began to think about her own mother, and how happy she used to be on Christmas morning, being allowed to get up in her nightdress to have a cup of tea and toast by the fire with her mother, and Twm in his bed at that time, as he certainly would be today, lying in after the binge of the previous night. But she did not care about it at that time, her mother was there, pretty and clean, and a shelter to her from any blow. It did not matter how poor they were because of Twm's wastefulness. That sun was there in her life, and had risen again by now in Begw's house; and her place in the town was safe if she went on as she was, and her master had praised her today.

As she thought of that she had an idea. She got hold of an old skirt and bodice of Lisi Jên's, and a rough apron: she lit a candle: she went to the kitchen and emptied the ashes, which had not been cleared for three days. She cleared the ashes from the hole under the oven too, which would have been there since the last baking day. She took the ashes out to be sieved in the starry darkness. She blackleaded the grate; she went to the cowshed to fetch some kindling of heather, and lit the fire. She boiled water and washed the floor, and the floor of the dairy. She dusted the furniture and polished it as best she could after her step-mother's neglect. How brightly her mother would polish them! But now she was not so depressed as when she was in bed. She went to look for a table cloth to put on the table, not a very clean one. But before eating in the light of the candle, she cleaned the glass of the lamp, glass which had been blackened by the smoke of the wick. She cut the wick even - it was no wonder that the kitchen was like a cellar when she came to the house last night. She cleaned the glass but it was not as shining as that of Elin Gruffydd which was shiny enough to brighten a chapel.

And there, in the comparative peace of the kitchen, she sat at the table and enjoyed a cup of tea and a slice of bread: she was once again a little girl, eight years old, having breakfast with her mother. But before she had quite finished Sionyn came down from the bedroom and shouted rudely,

'I want a present.'

There's a lot of his father in this little bully, thought Winni. She gave him the donkey and left him to play by the fireside. Then she made a fire under the oven ready to make dinner, without being quite sure if there was any meat. But she remembered seeing a parcel under her father's arm last night. She peeled the carrots and potatoes. The meat was beginning to sizzle when Lisi Jên got up, some time after nine. Winni's energy was surging through her body like a torrent of hot water.

'You're making dinner very early,' was Lisi Jên's first remark.

'The sooner we'll get it over. I don't know if you've got any pudding.'

'I made some yesterday.'

Lisi Jên enjoyed her breakfast down to the last crust before putting the pudding to re-boil, and before dressing Sionyn.

Twm got up by dinner time, he was half dressed, and had a dirty old handkerchief round his neck. He scowled at the dinner as if it had just quarrelled with him. He threw an occasional glance at his wife as he gulped the food down.

'And you've become too much of a lady there in the town to speak to your father,' was his first greeting to Winni, 'and wearing your best frock for dinner.'

'Yes, I want to be more of a lady if this is how it is to be common.'

'Who brought you up I wonder?'

'Not you, you old misery.'

'Leave him alone. said Lisi Jên, 'We'll have nothing but nagging all day. It's Winni who's made the dinner' she told her husband.

'So she should, its an honour for her to look after her father.'

There was a kind of devilish animal look about him at that minute, so that his daughter would have liked to strangle him and crush his flesh until he was squashed like bad potatoes boiled for the pigs. But just as in the town, something made her stop herself - perhaps because she was going to Begw's house for tea. Doing that to him would have spoiled her tea for her.

It was no surprise to Elin Gruffydd to see Winni and

Sionyn there before the others got back from the Literary Meeting. She remembered that Winni would not go to the festival after her mother died. The Literary Meeting was something with which one grew up over the years. Sionyn brought his donkey with him, and it kept him happy until tea time and prevented him from pestering Begw's youngest brother.

'I've made you another frock Winni, from the top of a piece I bought very cheaply in the market. That one will fall to bits if you don't have another one to change into.'

'Oh, isn't it pretty, Elin Gruffydd,' said Winni as she gazed at the red dress that she had put on, 'I can never thank you enough. I'll keep it on to have tea.'

'You'll have to have a coat for next winter too, but Lisi Jên should buy that out of your wages.'

'Yes, it's difficult to know what to do. My father was there when I had them last time, and I'd be in trouble if I didn't give them to him.'

'It's not my place to interfere; if I were to buy you clothes out of your wages Twm would give me a bad name in the quarry. And you know what that would mean. He might as well stand on a stall in the square and carry on about me from there. Couldn't you tell your master and mistress, they could refuse to give your wages to your father?'

'I'll try.'

The others came to the house from the meeting and ran to warm themselves by the fire, and Begw looked admiringly at Winni's new frock.

'Oh, you are pretty Winni.'

'Thanks to your mother.'

The tea was very plain, only bread and butter and jam, and home made bara brith with thick butter on it; but it was a feast to Winni to have it like this on a clean table, and everyone kindly. She was ashamed of Sionyn's frock and coat, although she had ironed them before coming; they were crumpled as if the dogs had been lying on them before that.

'How are things going in the town Winni,' asked Begw.

'Oh, the place is alright, plenty of style, plenty of carrying food upstairs, and plenty of work with the little boy.'

'He'll grow up, and summer will come.'

Winni began to laugh.

'Do you know, here's a funny thing.'

She stopped.

'Do you know what mince pies are?'

'No,' said the mother, 'I was in service on farms.'

'Well, you make pastry like for an apple tart, but you put it in little tins instead of on a plate, and you put this mince meat in the middle. And as the mistress was making the mince meat with apples, suet, raisins and that sort of thing, I asked her where was the meat, and the mistress really laughed. There's no meat in it.' 'Is it nice?' asked Robin. 'Lovely.' She began to laugh again. 'Think of Lisi Jên, the greatest slut, but she can make marvellous pastry. Isn't it strange that even useless people can do one thing well?' Everyone laughed.

'Well, I watched Lisi Jên making pastry. Twm Ffinni Hadog likes apple tart better than anything, in spite of his name, and I learned to make pastry. The mistress praised me.'

'You can make some for me next time.'

'I will if I'm still in the town.'

'Aren't you happy there Winni?'

'Oh yes,' she said thoughtfully.

Sionyn began to carry on about going home, and the smile left Winni's face.

'Look', said Elin Gruffydd, 'run home with him and come back for supper. I'm sure he wouldn't go with one of us.'

Winni cheered up again, and she was in high spirits when she returned. She had begun to get a taste for talking with adults by now, and these were good listeners. Begw was far from her, in a different world, the world of a child still. She felt that she was a woman by now, and if Begw were to be asked, she would say that this was not the same Winni who used to preach eloquently on the mountain; who stole her sandwiches from her basket, and danced barefoot. She had been tamed since then.

But one day she would grow up to Winni's age, and be her equal. At this time she could do nothing but listen in admiration. To the others, it was clear Winni was beginning to rise above her slum background.

'You were asking just now,' said Winni, as she enjoyed her supper of cold beef, pickled onions and cold Christmas pudding,

'Was I happy in my place? Yes, I am, but it's a very inconvenient old house there, I have to take every meal upstairs, and there's no bathroom there. So I have to carry water up to the living room when they want a bath.

They're talking about building a house outside the town, but this one is handy near the shop.'

She began to laugh, laughing so much that Begw laughed with her because she knew that something funny was coming.

'What do you think, the master washes the mistress in the bath there, I'd be ashamed for anyone to see me stark naked like that.' Elin Gruffydd began to perspire, and look at Robin, and a nervous embarrassment came over Begw. Elin Gruffydd cut across Winni.

'They say that your mistress is a very delicate woman, and has a lot of rheumatism, that's why, I'm sure.'

41

John Gruffydd put his spoke in.

'Were there many in the brake last night?'

'It was full, and everyone except me, and that man who gave me a shilling, had been drinking.'

'Yes, Elis Ifans the Wern; he had a subject for a sermon there I'm sure.'

'Do you know Guto Sboncyn?' asked Winni.

'Yes. I know him well.'

'Guto Grasshopper my father calls him when he has something bad to say about him. He was there. He hasn't got one tooth in his head; and when he was singing away and throwing back his head, you could see to the bottom of his stomach. Then he would go quiet and close his eyes, then he would look just like a carved image asleep.'

They had to laugh in spite of themselves.

The word 'carved' made Elin Gruffydd change the conversation.

'Do you go to Sunday School Winni?'

'Yes, every Sunday, but I have to rush home to make tea, so I don't see much of the girls in the class. We're a mixed lot, girls in service from the country like me, and town girls. You should hear the town girls putting on a posh accent, and they don't know anything about the Bible; they would talk about their sweethearts all through the lesson if they had the chance. But I don't want to talk about the town, I'm here tonight. Tomorrow night there'll be tramping feet over my head again.'

She became sad again, and sighed.

She did not see her father after going home, nor before leaving the following morning. He was enjoying part of his working shift in bed - less money for Lisi Jên at the end of the month. Lisi Jên would suffer one day, thought Winni, but she had got up to make breakfast for her. Sionyn was in a world of dreams and illusion.

On this grey dreary morning, just before dawn broke, a morning which could not raise anyone's hopes, on her way down to the town, Winni looked ahead to the future. She was determined to make her fortune; her purse was tied round her neck, and there were three pennies in it. Elin Gruffydd's new frock was in a parcel under her arm, and in her heart was the memory of the happy time yesterday with Begw's family.

*Chapter 4*

# Starting to Live

Deina Prys sat in the armchair by her hearth in front of a big blazing peat fire, day-dreaming and looking at her work. She had finished for the day. The surface of the table had been scrubbed clean with white grit, and the same grit had been scattered on the earth floor. The dresser, the linen press, and the clock had been polished until they shone. These stood on a slate platform and there were pictures of fish carved on the front of it. Deina took a pride in her oak furniture; she had an oak chest and table in the bedroom too, all of which had come from her old home at the far end of the parish, Pant y Llyn. Harri, her husband had been able to save enough money to buy chairs, tables and other things for the kitchen. A small spinning wheel stood on the floor, and with this she had spun linen curtains to put on the window.

She was twenty years old, and she had been married for a fortnight. It would be about four hours before her husband came home from the quarry, and she had nothing to read. There had not been many books in her old home, 'Y Bardd Cwsg' (The Sleeping Bard) and 'Llyfr y Tri Aderyn' (The Book of the Three Birds). But she had started knitting a pair of stockings, and her thoughts ran along with the wool. Her mind went back to the day when Harri came to Pant y Llyn as a farmhand. She loved him the first minute she saw him, when she was sixteen and he was eighteen. He was a sturdy boy, with warm brown eyes, reddish hair. a finely shaped head, good teeth, and weather-beaten skin. She used to go out into the farmyard at every opportunity so as to see him and talk to him. He used to pass her shyly with his head down, until one day she ventured to speak to him, and asked boldly whether he could read and write. When he answered that he could not and would give anything to be able to learn, she said that she would ask her father if he might come to the house so that she could teach him. (She and her sisters had had a little schooling with a spinster in the town.) She got permission, and then she taught him to read, with the Testament in front of him. In front of him also were pieces of old papers and a goose quill so that he could learn to form the letters. She was in heaven, just being able to look at him, although he used to smell of the stables. She wanted to take his hand and tell him that she liked him, but her sisters Grasi and Elizabeth were watching every move she made and sometimes her father too.

Harri slept in the loft above the stables and there was no chance to see him at night after the lessons finished. Sometimes she longed to go up to the stable loft, but she would never hear the end of it from her sisters if she went. She caught a glimpse of him during the day at mealtimes when the farmworkers came into the kitchen. At these times, she had noticed that Leusa the maid hovered around Harri waiting on him, and jealousy came to her heart. She decided that she would have to tell him that she loved him; and one day when she met him in the yard she told him. He bent his head and said huskily that he loved her too. She was in paradise after that, although she had only an occasional brief word with him in the yard.

Her sisters noticed these chats and took her to task, saying that she should not be keeping company with a servant, and that it would not be proper for the daughter of a farm like Pant y Llyn to marry a farmhand. She had told them plainly enough that she would marry no-one else. They were quite a bit older than she was, and Deina told them that they would be old maids all their lives if they waited expecting someone better. But the great thing was that she loved Harri, her sisters could never turn her away from that.

But something happened which made the two of them see each other less frequently. There was talk of a number of men going to open a quarry on the side of the mountain, three miles away and Harri began to take an interest in it and to go on Saturday evenings to see some of these people. The end of it was that he left Pant y Llyn and joined these men. Her father had done all he could to get him to stay, given him more wages, and a better place to sleep, since he was such a good worker. But Harri preferred more freedom and more adventure. His going was a great loss.

Deina found it very awkward now that she was not able to see her sweetheart about the farmyard, and she had to think of some way of seeing him. He had sent to tell her where he was staying through one of the farmhands, and she decided to go there on a Saturday afternoon. She saw him before he started out on foot for the town. She had his company almost all the way home, and that afternoon he was able to tell her how much he loved her, and he said that they could get married when he had built a cottage for them to live in. They were earning good money by quarrying slate that was very near the surface and selling it to a man in Caer Saint, and sharing the money between the six of them. Her sisters told her off when she got home, but they did not succeed in preventing her from seeing Harri like this every Saturday afternoon. Her home was a miserable place by then, her mother had died, her sisters were unkind and her father was an unhappy man because of having lost his wife. Although he said nothing to oppose Deina's courtship, he said nothing to encourage her either, but looked mournfully at her. What with all this there was no pleasure for Deina in her home, but she felt a deep contentment by thinking all the time of Saturday. But Oh! a week was a long time.

Things went on like this for two years, and in the end Deina told her father and her sisters that she was going to get married. Grasi did not say much, but Elizabeth said,

'You've insisted on having him, you'll have to live with him now.' Tears came to her father's eyes when he said,

'I'd rather see you marrying a farmer's son, but it's your happiness that's important, and I hope you'll both be happy. Harri's a good worker.'

They were married in the church on a dark December morning. Grasi agreed to be a bridesmaid, and the farm bailiff to be best man, and her father stood at her side. Elizabeth came to the service. Harri had no family, he was a child of the workhouse.

Sitting by the fire here this afternoon Deina remembered small things about the service – the church cold and dark, the wax dripping down the side of the rush candle like a small waterfall, the long shadows across the altar, and the priest going through the service in a colourless monotonous voice. She wore a full black silk skirt with green stripes, a black velvet bodice, and her mother's paisley shawl. Harri wore a suit of homespun cloth, the tailor having come to Pant y Llyn to make it through the kindness of her father. Although everything in the church looked so dismal and cold, Deina's heart was burning with happiness because her dream had come true. They had a wedding breakfast at Pant y Llyn of boiled pork, carrots and potatoes, and rice pudding with plenty of eggs in it.

The two of them went to their new house that afternoon.

Going over these things in her mind now she smiled as she remembered the happiness that she had, as it were, taken from her family and found in Harri.

She got up suddenly and went to the cowshed to see the little calf, her father's gift. She felt that he was not getting a fair chance, being alone here, without his mother. But Harri had heard about a good heifer at the far end of the parish and he was going there the following Saturday to see her and perhaps buy her.

The calf pranced about when he saw her, and shook his head. She patted him and gave him her hand to lick. She doted on him, and blushed to think that she was behaving like a child, and she a married woman now. This was how she used to play with every calf when she was a child.

Mist was swirling around the house, and through it she saw a woman coming through the gate, a basket on her arm and a pitcher in her hand.

'You don't know me?' she said as she strode towards the house. 'I'm Marged Huws, Twll Mawn, and I thought I should come and see how you are since you're a stranger here. I heard that you haven't got a cow yet and I've brought a small 'print' of butter, some barley bread and some buttermilk for you.'

'Well thank you very much, I'm very glad to see you. No-one has been near the house here since Harri went to the quarry. I just went to see the calf because I was fed up of being in the house with nothing to do.'

'You'll see more people in a while, when they've finished building the chapel, but perhaps you'll want to go down to your old church.'

'No, I'll go wherever Harri wants to go, and according to him he'll be going to the chapel.'

'They're going to try and get John Jones, Talysarn here

to open the chapel. We've become like heathens up here now; everyone feeling it's too far to go to the church.'

'You're not much better off for having been to church,' said Deina, 'the vicar there's hopeless, and half the service is in English and no-one can understand it. Hardly anyone who lives around here goes there now. I'm going to make a cup of tea for us; I had a bit from my sister, she got it from a wealthy friend from Anglesey.'

'It's very expensive, a real treat for us quarrying people.'

They had barley bread and oatcakes with the tea.

'Lovely', said Marged Huws, 'tea fit for the queen. You'll make Harri a good wife, and he's a hard-working lad. I don't know how it will be now after the change in the quarry. You see, before the men used to work co-operatively and share the profit. They had hard work getting rid of the heather to get down to the slate; and they had to have horses and carts to take the slates down to the town and sell them to a man there who sent them on somewhere else. But since this new man has bought the quarry they get wages.'

'Well, yes, and Harri gives most of his to me. He complains that this new man wants to make a profit and is driving them hard. He's going down and opening new levels in the rock.'

'Yes, it's a dangerous place now. But what am I doing talking like this to someone young. This mist will clear, and spring will come, and what a view you'll get from the sea and Anglesey.'

Deina enjoyed the conversation and enjoyed looking at Marged Huws. She had a kindly face, and only one tooth in her head. She was a woman of about forty, but looked much older.

She wore clogs and white stockings, a homespun petticoat and dress, a blue and white check apron, a shawl over her shoulders, a white frilled cap, and a small black hat on her head.

Deina felt happy after her visit, and more of a wife for having made tea for a neighbour. She hoped some others would come to visit her. She was glad to have the milk and butter. She got on with making a mash for the calf with the buttermilk; that would save Harri some work when he got home. Then she started to make a quarryman's supper; she put a saucepan full of potatoes in their jackets on the peat fire, and it sparked at being moved. Presently Harri would be home, and it would be so nice to forget what had happened at Pant y Llyn before her marriage, and be able to talk all evening with Harri.

*Chapter 5*

# Maggie

Dafydd Tomos and his son sat by the hearth on a warm evening in August. They had just finished supper, and tonight they had had tongue, to celebrate good news. They had had a bit of trouble for two months now; Sion and his father were out of work, the father for nearly a year, and Sion since he came home from college about two months ago. Sion had had work on the buses, but had given it up. One Saturday night, a gang of drunken youths came on the bus. One of them refused to pay for his ticket, and when Sion argued with him the youth hit him on the nose and mouth. Fortunately he did not lose any teeth but his nose bled very badly. His father said that he was not to go back after that, but his mother wanted him to go, rather than lounge about the house, as she said. Sion himself had no desire to go back, and to tell the truth he was afraid. Also he wanted a rest after the hard work of the examinations.

It was not so with the father although for the first fortnight he was glad to have time to work in the garden; the garden became too tidy, like the house in the hands of Maggie his wife. After that he saw time like a great calm sea before him.

The unemployment payment was a lot less than his wages at the factory, but he did not worry greatly about that.

There was no need now to pay for Sion at college, and he had a substantial nest egg in the bank. Neither he nor Maggie needed clothes. The thing which worried him was the endless monotony. Sometimes he would go out to the town square intending to have a chat with some of his friends, but they did not have much to say apart from complaining about the government. That did not have any effect on the government. He did not enjoy going for a walk. Nature meant nothing to him except for that which he saw in the garden.

But Sion was different. There was nothing he liked better than to go for a walk along the local footpaths. He liked to look at the mountains which surrounded the valley. He liked to look at them in the summer when the shadows ran over them. He liked to see them in the purple tranquillity of December. The flush of the sun as it set brought a kind of quietness to his heart. He liked to see the sheep and lambs in the fields nibbling the grass as if there were a machine in their mouths, but recently the thing which gave him the greatest pleasure, was Mot, the dog from next door, following him on his walks. Mot's pleasure was his pleasure. It was easy to see that the dog thoroughly enjoyed himself running and prancing and lifting his leg. He came to Sion's house every morning and sat like a carved image on the doorstep. When someone opened the door Mot would run and lie at Sion's feet for a while. Then he would begin to whine and Sion knew the meaning of that whining; he had to go for a walk with him, an activity which was neglected by his owners. Sion would be reluctant to start, but once he was out of the house he forgot his reluctance as he saw the effect on the dog. In spite of being out of work, those days were pleasant days.

However the pleasant days did not continue for long. Maggie began to behave very strangely. Dafydd Tomos and

Sion would like to laze for a while in their chairs and have a smoke after breakfast. However, Maggie began to shoo them out almost before they had finished eating, and to say that she wanted to get on with her work, and before anyone could say 'Jack Robinson', the chairs would be on the table and the carpet sweeper fetched from the back kitchen. The result of this was that Dafydd and Sion went to wash the dishes expecting that the chairs would be in their places by the time they finished. But no, they would be on the table, and Maggie would have gone upstairs to make the beds. There was no place for either of them to sit down, and they would go out, Sion with the dog and Dafydd to the town or the garden. Sometimes the chairs would not be in their places when they returned. This went on every day and Maggie began to complain.

'Go out somewhere and get out of my way. And it's high time that dog went home instead of leaving his dirty paw marks all over the floor.'

'His paws aren't dirty,' said Sion, 'and he'll go home when he's had a walk.'

'His place is in his home, not here, and he smells.'

'You're mistaken Mam, they wash him every week.'

'Oh well, this isn't his place. If they want to keep a dog let them keep him in their own house.'

Another trouble came. Who arrived there one day but Elsi, a student from the same year as Sion at college, who had come to stay with her aunt in the village. Elsi very soon discovered that Sion went for a walk with the dog every morning, and very soon she joined him. Sion did not have much to say to her.

'I'm sure your father and mother are glad to see you at home,' said Elsi.

'I don't know, my father is, but I don't know about my mother.'

'Why?'

'She's behaving very strangely, starting the cleaning almost before my father and I have finished breakfast.'

'Is she worried?'

'I expect so. There's a bit of a difference between the factory money and the dole.'

'That's what my father says.'

'Is he out of work?'

'Yes, since a year and a half. But my mother was very glad to see me come home. Look at that dog enjoying himself.'

'It's good that someone or something is happy. I haven't been happy these last few days.'

And in that way every day, the conversation would turn to Maggie's behaviour. One morning Elsi said;

'I've had good news from my mother this morning.'

'That's good.'

'My father's got a job.'

'New work?'

'No, he can go back to his old place in the factory.'

'That's lucky, I'd be glad if that were to happen to my father. I don't care about myself.'

'Forgive me for telling you', said Elsi, 'I see a strange look about your mother this time. Last year she was very welcoming to me. This year she hardly says anything.'

'Don't worry, she's odd with us too.'

'I remember someone the same in our village and she had to go to hospital.'

Elsi realised that she had made a mistake and became quiet.

In the house things went from bad to worse. Maggie objected to Elsi calling.

'She has her eye on you,' said Maggie.

'I can't help that.'

'You should tell her straight not to come after you.'

'I can't do that.'

'You can't I know only too well, men are too weak for anything now. They're too weak to get work.'

'You can't get work, Mam, if there's no work to be had.'

'There's plenty of work to be had.'

Sion saw that there was no point in arguing, and thought of Elsi's words about the woman who went to hospital. As the time went on Maggie stopped preparing dinner, and very often the chairs would be on the table when they returned to the house at mid-day. Dafydd and Sion would be forced to make dinner with whatever they found in the pantry.

One morning, after putting the chairs on the table Maggie began to carry on about Elsi, and to say that if Elsi came near the house again she would hit her. Then she began to bang the chairs on the floor and to shout, 'that dog gets more attention than I do.' Sion went out to telephone for the doctor and Mot had a short walk along the street instead of along the pleasant footpaths.

The result was that Maggie had to be taken to the hospital. Mot had a ride there in a bus every visiting day. But strangely enough when they went to tie him to the gatepost he would object, but would be quiet when Sion and his father returned. In contrast to her behaviour when she was at home Maggie became completely silent. She did not say a word to either of them when they went there, and they went home feeling sad. They found only one comfort. People were very kind to them. Every day Mot's owners would make them a good dinner. They managed as best they could with the other meals.

And tonight, when they were in the hospital, Maggie began to speak through her tears.

'I want to come home. I want to see Mot, the dear little dog.'

And that is why they had tongue for supper.

*Chapter 6*

# Emptiness

SUNDAY: Feeling irritated. Woken from a deep sleep at 6.30 a.m. Cannot understand why we have to be woken so early. Have a bit of a wash. Must wash my ears after going home. Try to eat my porridge without dropping any on the bed. The porridge is good, soft, and not one hard lump. Fail to eat the bacon and egg tidily. Forced to have help cutting the bacon. Even so, eat it messily. Try to dress myself. Succeed without the help of a nurse after a great effort. Feel proud because I have succeeded. Nice to be able to sit in the chair. A good dinner of lamb, carrots and potatoes, really good. Creamy rice pudding and apples. Try to read but fail. A lot of visitors in the afternoon. Feel that my head is empty. O.M. comes here after tea. She has a lot of cakes for me. The nurse puts them in the fridge. She and her husband and the children are very kindly. Feel lonely after everyone has gone, but no desire to read. Must do something to fill the time. Look out at the houses, every one of them someone's home. Long for my own comfortable home. Have supper of cold meat and salad and then go to bed. Have a sleeping tablet. So good to be able to sleep through the night and be able to close my eyes on pain.

MONDAY: The morning again the same. Have trouble dressing myself. Orders from the top that no-one is to help me, so that I will get used to it. A good dinner again of sausages and potatoes boiled white, rhubarb pudding and yellow sponge on top of it. Must do something about this emptiness. I tried to read today but failed. I have no interest in the television and when there is something interesting on in Welsh there is too much talking in the ward for me to be able to hear it. Although most of them can speak Welsh the rest have no interest in a Welsh programme.

Mrs. N. brings a book for me. I try to read it but cannot get beyond the second page. Have some of O.M.'s nice cakes for tea, and enjoy them. The nurse tells me off for standing instead of sitting while she makes the bed. Feel depressed. But another nurse comes to talk to me and says that she has had the same illness as me some years ago, and that she had recovered well after six months. She is very likeable and made me happy. That is how it is in the hospital here: there are many nurses who are agreeable and kind but there are some who can be nasty.

In spite of everything boring in my life I am thinking, but my thoughts have not got very far; they turn on one spot round the little things which happen in the hospital here. Sometimes there is a variation, such as this morning when a minister came here to give us communion. Feel sad to look at the handful of old people, no-one young amongst them. At the end one old woman, 93 years old, going up to the minister and saying, 'Isn't Wales a lovely country?' I could laugh to think of the contradiction, and the observation gives me something to think about for a while. And here I am getting an idea, what if I were to make up a story in my head to fill this emptiness and prevent me from longing too much for my home. It had to be a story about young people, and tonight my mind is full of the story.

TUESDAY: But today my mind is filled with something else. It is, or it was, a woman, not as old as the rest of us, suffering with something on her breast. When we were having dinner there was a bit of a noise in her throat. The nurses came with my dinner, and suddenly the noise in the next bed quietened. Two nurses went to her. Then I saw the two running off with a gesture to me: I understood the meaning of the sign; the woman had died. We had to go to the day room, and we were there for two hours, conscious of the commotion going on, the doctors and the nurses rushing about. Deeply upset, I cannot think of anything except this woman who was alive beside me one minute, and the next minute was dead. How small the border is between being alive and being dead. I did not have the second lot of O.M.'s cakes for tea today. Not one left.

WEDNESDAY: Everything going on the same way. Wake up, bit of a wash, breakfast, dress myself. (Had a bit of quiet help from a nurse today and I was so grateful.) I cannot drag my mind away from the woman yesterday; no-one from outside comes to the ward today. Orthopaedic specialist comes in the afternoon. Looks agreeable, a tall man, dark haired. English by his accent. He put his hand affectionately on my head and I had a sensation of happiness. He did not say much, only told me to get well soon. After a while I was full of the story, and this is what went through my head.

'Jane was 25 years old and had never been in love. She saw no-one to whom she felt she could entrust her life. She was not one who wanted to go out with boys , and say like her friends that she had a 'boyfriend', as the contemporary newspapers usually put it. She wanted someone whom she could consider marrying. She worked in an office and she had a good job. Although she had been to college she did not want to become a teacher. She had taken some notice of the minister of the Independent Chapel in the town, and had had an occasional talk with him, but without thinking any more of it, only that he was a sensible man with good conversation. His name was Wiliam Richards, a man of about 30, not tall, fair haired, an interesting face, not too good-looking, but very kind. It was his kindness which made her enjoy talking to him in the street.

One night the front doorbell of her lodgings rang, and her landlady brought Mr. Richards to her room. She asked him to sit down on the sofa, and she sat beside him, one of those impulsive things she sometimes did. Having talked for a while he suddenly said, 'Could you marry a minister?' She answered just as suddenly, 'I could if he was like you.' At that he took her in his arms and kissed her. She felt a thrill go down her spine and she knew from that minute that she loved him.'

That is as far as I could go today, but my mind was so full of the story that I had to go back over it, I do not know how many times. I could not write it down, I was too tired, but as I went over it Jane and I became one, I took her place.

THURSDAY: Although I enjoyed making up a story in my head yesterday, I had a fit of depression today. Looking out of the window at the trees and thinking of my garden at home. The lilac tree was flowering abundantly and I could not see it. A desperate longing came over me and I did not have the heart to go on with the story. Feel that I am a nuisance to everyone and that I might as well die; it would be no loss.

But that feeling was only for a minute; I wanted to live, and my enthusiasm for the story came back. I wanted the company of my friends again, and to enjoy life in their company. A little nurse came to me, a very sweet one, when I was on the way to the toilet, and asked if she could help me. I accepted gladly because she was so nice.

E. came here in the afternoon and I was very glad to see her, not having seen her for a long time. We did not have a lot of time to talk intimately because some other visitors arrived, and for once I felt that it would be better if they did not give permission for visiting at all times. E. gave me plenty of stamps as a present, very convenient things as there are some letters I must answer. The eagerness to go on with the story came back to me after E. had gone. (The other visitors had the sense to go before her.) E. keeps her age well and is still attractive. I went on with the story but not before I had been over the part I made up yesterday, that is, in my mind.

'Jane and Wiliam were quiet after the kiss, but presently he said,

'I'd like to get married soon.'

'Wait until we get to know one another better,' she said.

'I feel as if I've known you for a hundred years, and I love you.'

'Since when?'

'For ages, speaking to you in the street I'd say to myself, 'That's the wife for me.'

'But you must remember that marrying a minister is a very important step. If we were to make a mistake it wouldn't be easy to get a divorce.'

'But why are you talking about a divorce almost before we start going together? I think I know you well enough to believe that that will never happen.'

'I'm just looking ahead to see what might happen.'

'Our wedding won't be a leap in the dark. Let's get engaged shall we?'

Jane agreed to that.'

FRIDAY: The official comes to tell me that I can go home next week, but I will have to have someone to look after me, or I will have to go to a nursing home, and if that should happen I would have to sell my house. Feeling happy and downhearted, but feeling grateful that I am not like the old woman in the next bed. She does not talk to anyone, not even to the people who come to see her every day, the same people. When the nurse lifts her into the chair she screams with pain. Some nurses are impatient with her and the others make a fuss of her. Then she sits with her chin on her breast all day. A nurse has to feed her every meal. There is talk of moving her from here. Poor thing.

My thoughts are troubled, running between gladness at being allowed home and fear of being forced to go into a nursing home. I long to be able to go home. A feeling of envy comes over me when I hear the nurses here running back and fore so nimbly, and I am so feeble, with a stick. In the midst of this mental turmoil I am comforted by going back over my story from the beginning and continuing to put myself in Jane's place. But I must go on with it in spite of all my troubled thoughts.

'Jane and Wiliam went for walks on the mountains.

The two of them went out buy an engagement ring, with one sapphire in it. Jane felt doubtful for a minute, wondering whether she was doing the right thing. The life of a minister's wife was a hard one, as was the life of a minister himself for that matter. They had to try not to tread on the corns of so many different types of people, and keep the peace between them. It would always be 'The wise man keeps his peace.'

But in the shop, looking at Wiliam's kindly face Jane's heart gave a leap of joy. She could not disappoint him, he was so loveable. Yes she loved him deeply, and having put the ring on her finger she felt that she was already

61

married. She gave Wiliam a kiss in front of the shop-keeper.

The following Monday at the office she received congratulations from all directions. Everyone said that they were made for one another. She felt shy.

Wiliam came often to Jane's lodging, and since he was her landlady's minister, the latter showed no objection. They continued to walk the mountains pausing to sit now and again, and finishing in some town to have tea. The two were so loving towards one another that people turned to look at them. But they did not care. In the end Wiliam said that there was no sense in going on like this. It would be better to get married. Jane agreed.'

SATURDAY: My friends came here and said that they had heard of someone to look after me when I go home. Tears came to my eyes, not only because I can go home, but because I have such faithful friends. The story gave me the same pleasure again. Perhaps I would go on with it. I would go over it again and again in my mind, imagining still that I was the young Jane.

# Translator's Notes

Some of the characters in the first three stories here appeared in an earlier book by Kate Roberts – 'Te yn y Grug', 'Tea in the Heather', published in 1959.

In this earlier work, Winni, the main character here, was a child growing up in the late nineteenth and early twentieth centuries. She lived in one of the villages near Caernarfon where Kate Roberts herself grew up, and where most people survived by a combination of working in the slate quarries of Snowdonia, and scratching a living on smallholdings scattered on the thin soil and exposed mountain sides of this region. Winni was both neglected and abused. She was expected to work in the house, and given no education, guidance or even clothing. She was befriended by a younger child, Begw, and the girls used to wander the mountain side together.

Begw's mother, Elin Gruffydd, gave Winni what help and support she could, and when Winni reached her teens and was considered old enough, she found her a place in the town of Caernarfon where Winni took what was probably the only career option open to her, and went into domestic service. (As a young child Winni had fantasised about going into service with the Queen – Victoria.)

The three stories translated here focus on Winni and her family, her employers, and the family of her friend Begw, who gave her so much support.

They are as follows:

## Winni Ifans

**Twm Ifans:** A quarryman and Winni's father; also known as Twm Ffinni Hadog. In this area nicknames were not only commonplace (and colourful) but were often used as a substitute for a surname. In this way Winni, by association, became known as Winni Ffinni Hadog.

**Lisi Jên:** Winni's uncaring and slovenly stepmother.

**Sionyn:** Son of Lisi Jên and Twm Ffinni Hadog, half brother to Winni. He is between two and three years old.

**Begw:** Winni's friend, several years younger than she is.
**Elin Gruffydd:** Begw's mother. She befriended Winni and provided her with clothes to go to her first job.

**John Gruffydd:** Elin's husband, and father of Begw and Robin. A quarryman.

**Robin:** Begw's brother.

**Mr and Mrs Hughes:** Winni's employers. Owners of a shop in the town.

**Robert:** Their four year old son.

**Elis Ifans the Wern:** A lay preacher and neighbour from Winni's home village who comes to her assistance when her father takes all her wages.

The songs which are mentioned in the third story, 'My Grandma's Old Stick', 'The Little Thatched Cottage', and 'I Remember Now So Clearly', are songs which were popular in this part of the world in the late nineteenth and early twentieth centuries.
**The brake** which is mentioned several times was the precursor to the 'bus'; an open horsedrawn vehicle which conveyed people to and from the town. It was the only form

of transport available to the ordinary working people of the area.

The fourth story, 'Starting to Live', describes a young woman, Deina Prys, who is newly married, and living in the same quarrying and farming district where Kate Roberts herself grew up.

The books mentioned in this story are classics.

'**The Sleeping Bard**' is an abbreviation of 'Visions of the Sleeping Bard' by Ellis Wynne, first published in 1703. It consists of three visions; of the World's Course, of Death's lower Kingdom, and of Hell. The language of the book had a lasting influence on Welsh literary style.

'The Book of the Three Birds' was published by Morgan Llwyd in 1653, a time when the Civil War was over, Charles I had been executed, and Cromwell had assumed power as Lord Protector of the Commonwealth. The three birds of the title are used symbolically to represent Civil Power – the Eagle; the Royalists – the Raven; and the Puritans – the Dove, and their speech interprets the signs and events of the times, in particular as to how they relate to the spiritual life of the Welsh people.

The story, 'Maggie', is set later in the twentieth century in an anonymous suburbia, and deals with the themes of unemployment and the consequent mental and emotional distress.

'Emptiness', the last story, was written in Kate Roberts' old age.

CAROLYN WATCYN
*September 2000*